For Alice and Hélène, my two princesses.

For Zoé, my new little sweetie, my little doll.

P. L.

... Mona?!

... Nils! ...

Just wait a ... Nils! ... I ...

JUNE! I said n ... Niiiils! That's enough ... OK! Nils!

... That's enough now ... OK, Nils!

OK!

... NO DE-DI-CA-TION!

Phew!

R. D.

Cover:
Portrait of Princess Hot-Head with battle head-dress,
after her victory at the battle of Atalanta
Unknown, the Queens Museum of Princesses

STERLING and the distinctive Sterling logo are registered trademarks
of Sterling Publishing Co., Inc.

Library of Congress Cataloging-in-Publication Data Available

Lot#: 10 9 8 7 6 5 4 3 2 1
02/10
Originally published in 2004 as *Princesses oubliées ou inconnues*
by Hachette Livre/Gautier-Languereau
43 quai de Grenelle, Cedex 15, 75905 Paris, France
Published in English by Sterling Publishing Co., Inc.
387 Park Avenue South, New York, NY 10016
Translation © 2010 by Sterling Publishing Co., Inc.
Illustrations © 2004 by Rébecca Dautremer
Translated by Toula Ballas
Distributed in Canada by Sterling Publishing
c/o Canadian Manda Group, 165 Dufferin Street
Toronto, Ontario, Canada M6K 3H6
Distributed in the United Kingdom by GMC Distribution Services
Castle Place, 166 High Street, Lewes, East Sussex, England BN7 1XU
Distributed in Australia by Capricorn Link (Australia) Pty. Ltd.
P.O. Box 704, Windsor, NSW 2756, Australia

Printed in China
All rights reserved

Sterling ISBN 978-1-4027-6677-0

For information about custom editions, special sales, premium and
corporate purchases, please contact Sterling Special Sales Department
at 800-805-5489 or specialsales@sterlingpublishing.com.

Philippe Lechermeier · Rébecca Dautremer

the secret lives of
Princesses

STERLING

New York / London

www.secretlivesofprincesses.com

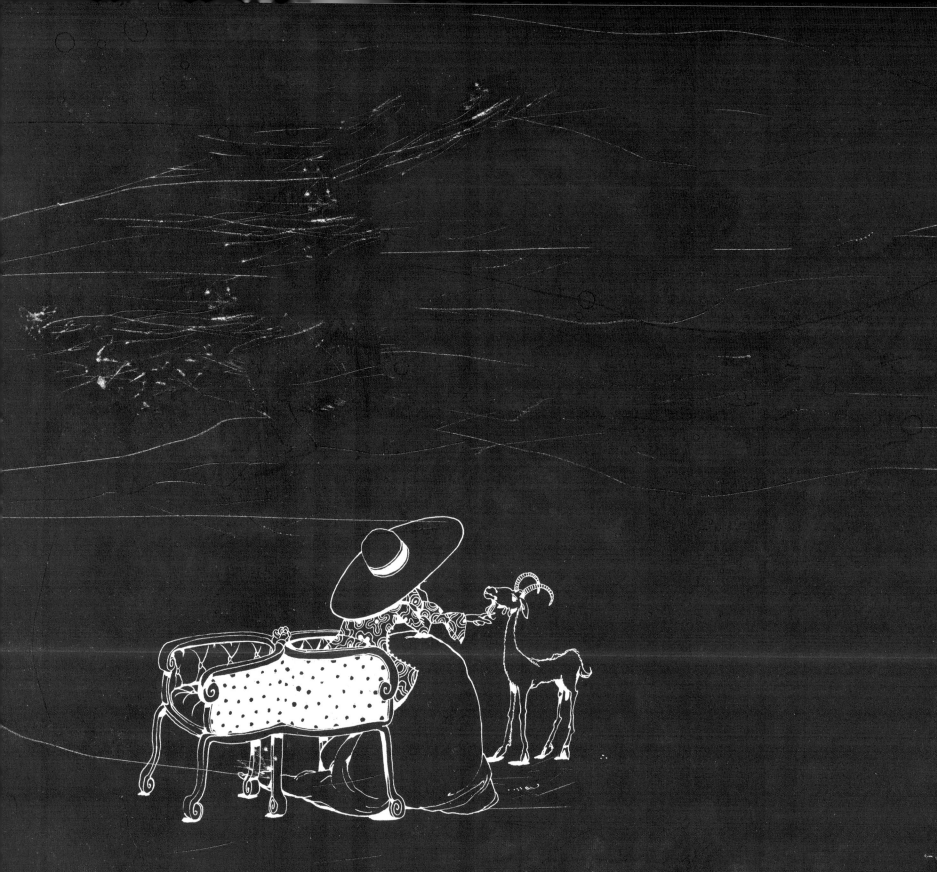

The sulking seat, formally known as the back-to-back. Perfect for small snits.
Available in plain and polka-dotted versions.
Owned by only the most refined princesses. for more details, see:

Have you spotted Princess Anne Phibian?
Chatted with Princess Babbling Brooke?
Stumbled upon the Night Princess?
Had a word with Princess Paige?
Crossed paths with Princess Picaresque or danced with
Princess Tangra-la around the campfire?
Princess Quartermoon, Princess Do-Re-Mi,
Princess For-a-Day ... they are too grand to stay concealed in the
back of a palace or at the top of a tower.
They have been hidden so well, some no longer even know
themselves.
But now all will be revealed—the behind-the-scenes
stories and secret lives of
the world's unknown, anonymous, and vanished princesses.
Mysterious mansions, corridor whispers, backroom confidences,
enchanted forests, murmured secrets, faithful pets—everything
will finally be explained.
And who knows, perhaps you might even recognize
yourself in these tales of long ago ...

The Cradle

The birth of a princess is a major event and the cause of many celebrations. Friends and family are all invited to visit the little one and bend over the cradle to ooh and aah. They come to offer their congratulations, and they each bring a nice little speech.

THE CLASSIC VERSION:
She will be the most beautiful princess in the world or She will be the most intelligent princess in the world.

THE OPTIMISTIC VERSION:
This princess will not be a chatterbox. (See also Tips and Techniques for Shushing a Princess, page 84.)

THE UNIQUE VERSION:
This princess will play the sousaphone.

THE BEST KNOWN VERSION:
In her fifteenth year, this princess will prick herself on a spindle and will drop dead.
(Fortunately, someone else adds: The princess doesn't really drop dead but actually falls into a deep hundred-year sleep.)

THE RADICAL VERSION:
This princess will ride a bike without using her hands.

THE SCHOLARLY VERSION:
She will never make spelling mistakes.

THE POETIC VERSION:
This princess will drink in the morning dew.
Nimble and light, she will bathe in the night
under the mists of the moon.

It is particularly **important** not to forget anyone, because **overlooked** guests can become quite **annoyed** if they are not part of the festivities.

One famous oversight occurred when **Sleeping Beauty's** parents forgot to send an invitation to a distant cousin who worked as a fairy. She was so offended by the blunder that she cast a spell on the princess. (You know the one.) The result: about a century of sleep.

It seems that Princess **Miss Hap's** legendary clumsiness was the result of a spell brought on by her parents' negligence. Consumed by greed, they limited the number of party guests so as not to be ruined by the catering costs. They regretted their stinginess for years to come (find out why on page 24).

THE GODMOTHER:
A figure chosen by parents to watch a princess. Has an overall tendency to spoil her charge. Always brings gifts and grants the most outrageous wishes. Cinderella's godmother, for example, was happy to help her transform a pumpkin into a carriage. However, despite the princess's pleading, she refused to convert a cat into a hat, a quail into a whale, or a guitar into a car.

GROWING A PRINCESS:
There is an age-old rumor which states that newborn princesses are dropped into rose bushes at midnight. Let's put a stop to that gossip right now. Children have the right to know the truth, so let's be clear about this: The only way to grow a princess is to plant one in the palace garden. See chart below for your seed preference.

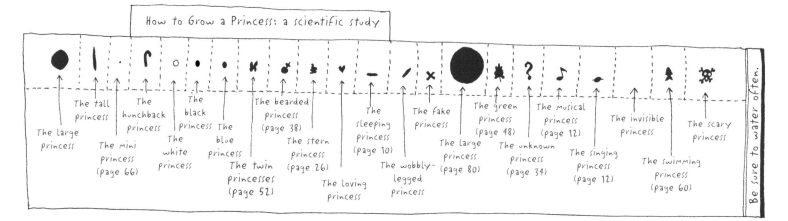

How to Grow a Princess: a scientific study

The large princess · The tall princess · The mini princess (page 66) · The hunchback princess · The white princess · The black princess · The blue princess · The bearded princess (page 38) · The twin princesses (page 52) · The stern princess (page 26) · The loving princess · The sleeping princess (page 10) · The wobbly-legged princess · The fake princess · The large princess (page 80) · The green princess (page 48) · The unknown princess (page 34) · The musical princess (page 12) · The singing princess (page 12) · The invisible princess · The swimming princess (page 60) · The scary princess

Be sure to water often.

Princess Somnia

Comes from a royal family of do-nothings.

Laziness is their policy,

and the sloth their emblem. Against the background of a

quilted comforter, their coat of arms declares their motto:

Be quiet—I'm sleeping.

There are no crowns in this family,

just nightcaps.

No dresses, only nightgowns.

Their ideal state is boredom.

Princess Somnia has one fast rule:

Do nothing which involves the slightest bit of effort. She goes

to bed early, gets up late, and never misses a chance to nap.

In between these moments of rest, in order to relax,

she curls up on enormous cushions of legendary softness.

IS RELATED TO:

Sleeping Beauty: Using the

excuse of a slight pinprick, she slept

for a hundred years and dragged

along her kingdom into

a deep slumber as well.

AND ALSO:

Princess PJ: never on her feet.

And Princess Snoozy-Q, who is

rarely seen.

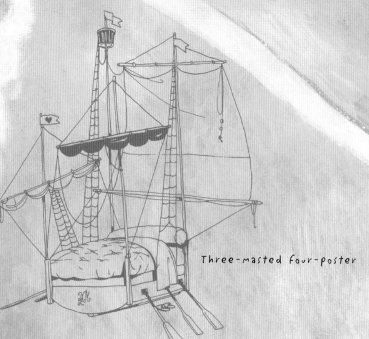

Three-masted four-poster

THE FOUR-POSTER BED:

A bed embellished with draperies. Perfect for sleepy princesses. Whether it's adorned with silk, lace, satin, or dragonfly wings, it's a classic look and an essential part of any bedroom.

The magic material that makes up the canopy is called the sky, and sometimes you can see stars make their nightly passage before your sleepy eyes.

You can find other four-posters which offer various options: the draperies on the *three-masted bed* can be turned into sails; the *free fall* is decorated with parachute cloth, in case of emergency landings; and the *open skies* is designed to be used outdoors on camping trips. Finally, there's the *super-extra-large king-size*, which is almost as big as a small palace and is covered with miles of blankets, duvets, and pillows.

Princess Do-Re-Mi

First violin in the royal court orchestra led by her husband, maestro Tempo Moderato.

Plays *pizzicato* when she's alone and *agitato* when she's angry.

And when she plays for her husband, sometimes she's often *affettuoso* and sometimes *amoroso*.

Princess Fa-Sol-La

The sister of the celebrated violinist Princess Do-Re-Mi, she is blessed with a crystal-clear voice and many admirers. Singing is her life. Why speak when one can sing? Why argue when one can practice scales? Grand arias burst forth when she's annoyed, delicate hymns when she is sad, and yodeling when she needs to chase away the blues.

When she laughs, glasses break, and when she cries, it's so moving that all the world applauds.

She spends her life at the opera and at concerts. And when the theaters are closed, she performs for very lucky private guests. Elegant and well-bred, she never utters a false note.

SO-SO OBOE:
A small woodwind instrument.

GRECO-ROMAN LUTE:
A no-holds barred instrument.

HORN OF PLENTY:
Available in fruit and vegetable varieties.

TWITTERER:
Babbling Brooke's instrument (see page 18).

WINKING VIOLIN:
Played by batting one's eyes.

JUMBO PICCOLO:
Played by Princess Buffet on gloomy days (see page 80).

TATTERED TRUMPET:
Only plays off-key.

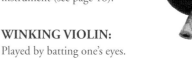

BUBBLE BASS:
A round and cumbersome instrument. Bumped into frequently.

CUCKOO HORN:
No practice required for this instrument. Blow anywhere, press anything, and let your hands do whatever they want.

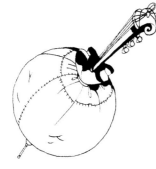

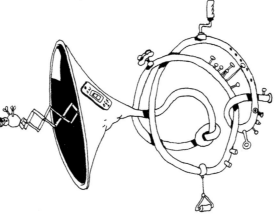

DANCE:

As everyone knows, princesses must learn to dance gracefully from a very young age. The worst possible insult for a princess is for people to say that she has two left feet. (In truth, most princesses have both a left and a right foot.)

When she's not in the rhythm and doesn't listen to the tempo, they say she's off-beat. But it's always hard to pay the piper when you just want to march to the beat of your own drummer.

The *minuet* is the most popular dance, but the *crossed quadrille* and the *arabesque* are also quite trendy. Then there are dances like the *bunny hop*, the *rumba*, and the *jitterbug*, in addition to the *jerk*, the *tango*, and the *fandango*.

There's also the dangerous *dragon dance*, the mysterious *dance of veils*, and the liveliest of all dances, the *shimmy-shake*. The *snobinella* is reserved for the most select princesses, of course.

For those wild and crazy nights, there's the *piggly-wiggle*, the *rug-cutter*, the *watusi*, and the *boogie-woogie*.

04 - VII - 04

14

To dance is to have winged feet.

Princess Tangra-la

Princess Tangra-la dresses wildly, without care,
in secondhand clothes from her head to her toes.

Some say she is dumpy, bedraggled, and frumpy. She just shrugs her shoulders. *Who cares?* She's too busy thinking about dancing.

She adores the *shindig* and the *hully-gully*,
while the *java* and *fiesta* couldn't be cooler.

Tangra-la lisps a little, which makes some meanies snicker. But she doesn't pay attention to their kind.

She surrounds herself with those who are definitely not ordinary.

Who wants to be among the plain and mundane?

Princess Paige

As soon as the ball is over or once the meal is done, Princess Paige scampers away and climbs the thousand steps which lead to her library.

She reads everything she can find: novels, poetry, philosophy, and tall tales.

She is also writing her autobiography. (She has finished three volumes and a total of five hundred and fifty-seven pages, covering only a small portion of her ten years.)

Her quest: to find the perfect pair of glasses.

She divides her days into chapters and dreams up titles for each one.

An expert in rhyme, she speaks only in verse. She knows the dictionary by heart.

A princess's teardrop.
Please do not blot.

Princess Alli Fabette

~~Prencess~~ Princess Alli Fabette is verry pritty butt

she has a huje problim:

she dusn't spell verry welll.

TEARS:
A princess's tears
are prized the world over.
For centuries, caravans and traders
traveled across sand and sea
looking for this rare find.
Like invisible ink,
they are used to compose
the sweetest songs,
the most beautiful poetry,
and the most adoring love letters.
For break-up letters and insults,
use crocodile tears.

Princess Babbling Brooke

As talkative as a parrot and impossible to understand, she chatters about everything and says nothing. There's lots of blah blah blah and plenty of tralala.

Her conversations have neither head nor tail—it's all a mishmash, a muddle, and a hodgepodge. She begins at the end, mixes up names, and—even worse—

she says a lot of naughty words.

Holding a conversation with her is exhausting. Getting a word in edgewise demands great skill. She scares off all princes, from the most timid to the most brave. Even her parents avoid her. They fear for their eardrums.

However **troublesome** in times of **peace**, though, Princess Babbling Brooke is **appreciated** during times of **war**. Her terrible chattering is quite useful in forcing soldiers to run off into battle when they lack courage. And, as effective as a cannon, her babbling has been known to cause even the boldest enemies to flee.

Was awarded the Medal of Grit for her bravery. (see page 82)

FAN:

A fan is a very useful object.
Speak directly into it while revealing
your secrets and your voice will
be disguised.

THE INTERNATIONAL ALPHABET OF FANS

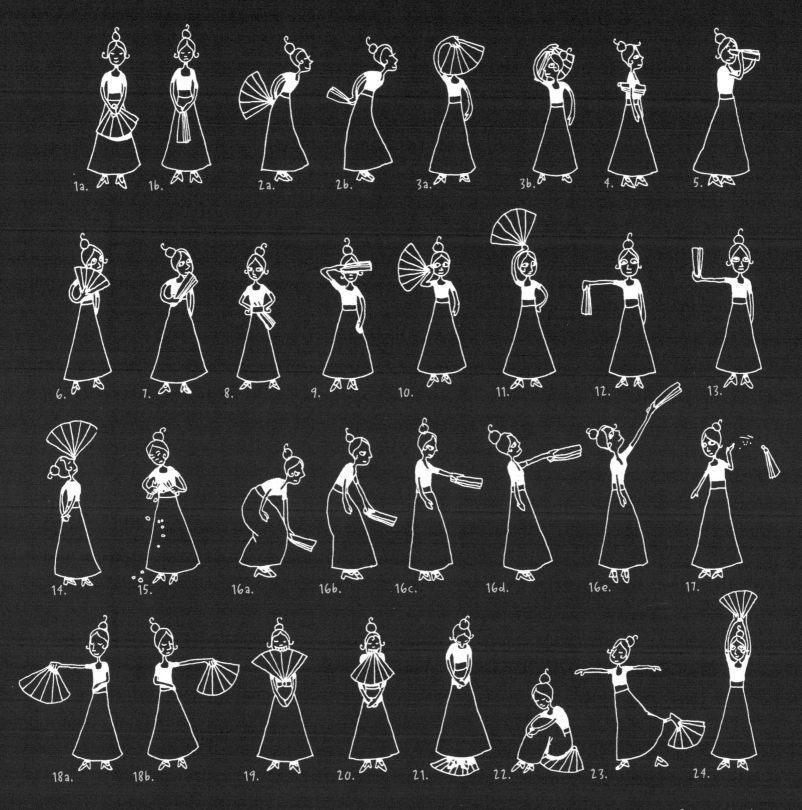

1a: Yes. – 1b: No. – 2a: Do you want to marry me? – 2b: Would you leave me alone? – 3a: What awful weather!
3b: What a beautiful day! – 4: I'm going out to buy bread. – 5: Which way is the exit? – 6: And why not?
7: Because. – 8: Are you causing trouble? – 9: I'm tired. – 10: Would you repeat the question?
11: What do you think of Molly Coddle's new hair style? (see next page) – 12: Below. – 13: Above.
14: I'm thinking of joining the circus. – 15: No, no, no, and no! – 16a: This prince is a complete dud!
16b: This prince is too small! – 16c: This prince is kind of short. – 16d: This prince is not too bad.

Princess Molly Coddle

Stubborn and difficult, Princess Molly Coddle doesn't speak, she whispers. She doesn't cough, she hacks. When presented with a fine meal, she barely touches it. At best, she'll have a nibble.

She's a real handful.

Princess Molly Coddle is frequently spoiled and never hesitates to demand the impossible: snow in the middle of summer, shade in the desert, and fresh blueberries in January.

She is most often found in her bath and expects all the details to be perfect: an ideal temperature, perfumed bath foam, rose petals, and apricot syrup.

Her cousin is the famous Princess of the Pea, whose story is well-known: The queen wanted to find the most refined bride for her son. When a lost young woman arrived at the castle one night, the queen slipped a pea under a mattress, and covered it with twenty more mattresses and twenty feather beds. After spending a night on the bed, Molly Coddle's cousin was so bothered by the pea she complained that she hadn't slept a wink. The queen knew she had found a rare and refined pearl and married her immediately to the prince.

But there's another version of this story that claims the princess was actually eaten by a giant who mistook her green gown for a delicious spring pea pod. Those who believe this story say that Princess of the Pea is therefore the name of a recipe. (*Royal Cuisine or How to Prepare a Princess: Twenty Simple and Savory Recipes*, page 79)

Another very distant cousin (thousands of miles distant) is Princess Kosekose (Japan, 6th century AD), who was a master of the tea ceremony and whose castle was surrounded by a natural hot spring, where she soaked much of the day.

ETIQUETTE:

Most princesses present themselves with courtesy and civility, respecting the rules of politeness and propriety. Some princesses, however, like to provoke scandals and keep tongues wagging. They enjoy pushing the boundaries of what is expected from a good princess. People still talk about Princess Oblivia who came to the ball without her dress, or Princess Meetu with her blue and red hair, or Princess Buffet, who fell asleep at the table with her head on her plate. (see Princess Oblivia, page 36; Princess Meetu, page 82; Princess Buffet, page 80) For further examples of poor princess etiquette, take note: It is impolite to eat with your feet on the table, ill-bred to stick out your tongue during the crowning of a new queen, and uncouth to pick your nose with the royal scepter.

Princess Miss Hap

Legendary throughout the world for her clumsiness, Princess Miss Hap always leaps before she looks.

She breaks all she touches and knocks over everything in her way. Living with her can be quite stressful. Even the prince she wanted to marry fell victim to her thoughtless ways, and was forced to leave after numerous unfortunate accidents: a broken arm, a crushed hand, and other situations too delicate to mention. For her own safety (and for the safety of others), she was sent to live on an island, away from anything (or anyone) she could break.

Miffed by this isolation, she sulked for several days— who could blame her?—but then began to devise plans for escape.

(see Voyages, page 44, and The Cradle, page 8)

24

THE SULKING SEAT:
A type of seat on which two princesses can sit and turn
their backs on each other.
In frequent use in most palaces, particularly those with
numerous princesses.
In particularly high demand when princesses are grumpy.
The china-silk sulking seat owned by the Flip-Flop
sisters is one of the most beautiful models. (see page 52)
The most elegant version belongs to Princess Molly
Coddle and is decorated in polka-dot fabric. (see page 22)
Some carriages come equipped with them, thereby
allowing princesses (and their families) to travel in peace.

TO SULK (VERB):
I sulk (rarely)
You sulk (don't you?)
She sulks (fairly common)
We sulk (admit it)
They sulk (too often)

Synonyms:
To brood, to be in a huff, to pout,
to act like a princess.

BOUDOIR (from the French verb *bouder*, to sulk):
A room of one's own. Perfect for feeling sorry for oneself.
Gets lots of use.

Example:
"I'm going to my boudoir."
"Why?"
"Because!"

DEGREES OF SULKING:
1. A snit: Momentary sulkiness
2. A huff: Deep sulkiness by a princess of some stature

Forgetting to smile is like forgetting to water the plants.

Princess Primandproper

Has a permanently pinched face.

Lacks all ability to bend.

Shows no trace of softness.

Is straight as an I

and always demands justice.

She rises very early each morning,

lunches and dines at the same time

each day, and cannot tolerate

any deviation,

lateness, or delay.

She hates whimsy,

idle chatter between friends,

and the slightest noise.

Her only passion: raising black butterflies.

(see Black Butterfly, page 62)

Her best friend: a wasp.

She always wears the same

outdated attire.

Doesn't laugh anymore because the last

time she did, her bun came undone, she tripped,

and her skirt flew up over her head.

Since that fateful day she has only worn pants.

Perfectly pressed pants.

Got married late in life to the Baron of Broken Hearts.

26

The Night Princess

The youngest daughter of the Night Queen and sister of the sweet and lovely Princess Pastel Pashmina.

She is jealous of her sister's fame and beauty and hates her with a passion. Her sister is luminous and light, while the Night Princess is somber and wicked. Pastel Pashmina loves the company of others.

The Night Princess lives far away from the gaze of people, deep in the shadow of a castle's tower.

She loves no one except her Siamese cat. She scares her own shadow.

Hide if you happen to see her some late evening in a corner of the hallway.

(see also The Garden, page 74)

The Faceless Princess

Always hidden, always camouflaged.

An expert in disguise, she can assume any appearance: a burglar, a spy, a pickpocket, or a forger. Nothing frightens her. Unrecognizable, no one ever knows where she is or what she looks like. Appears suddenly when least expected, always ready with a low blow. Most people count their blessings when she's not there.

She is good friends with most pirates.

THE INVISIBLE PRINCESS

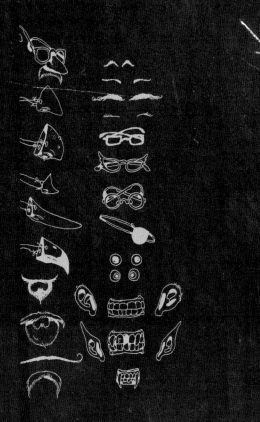

28

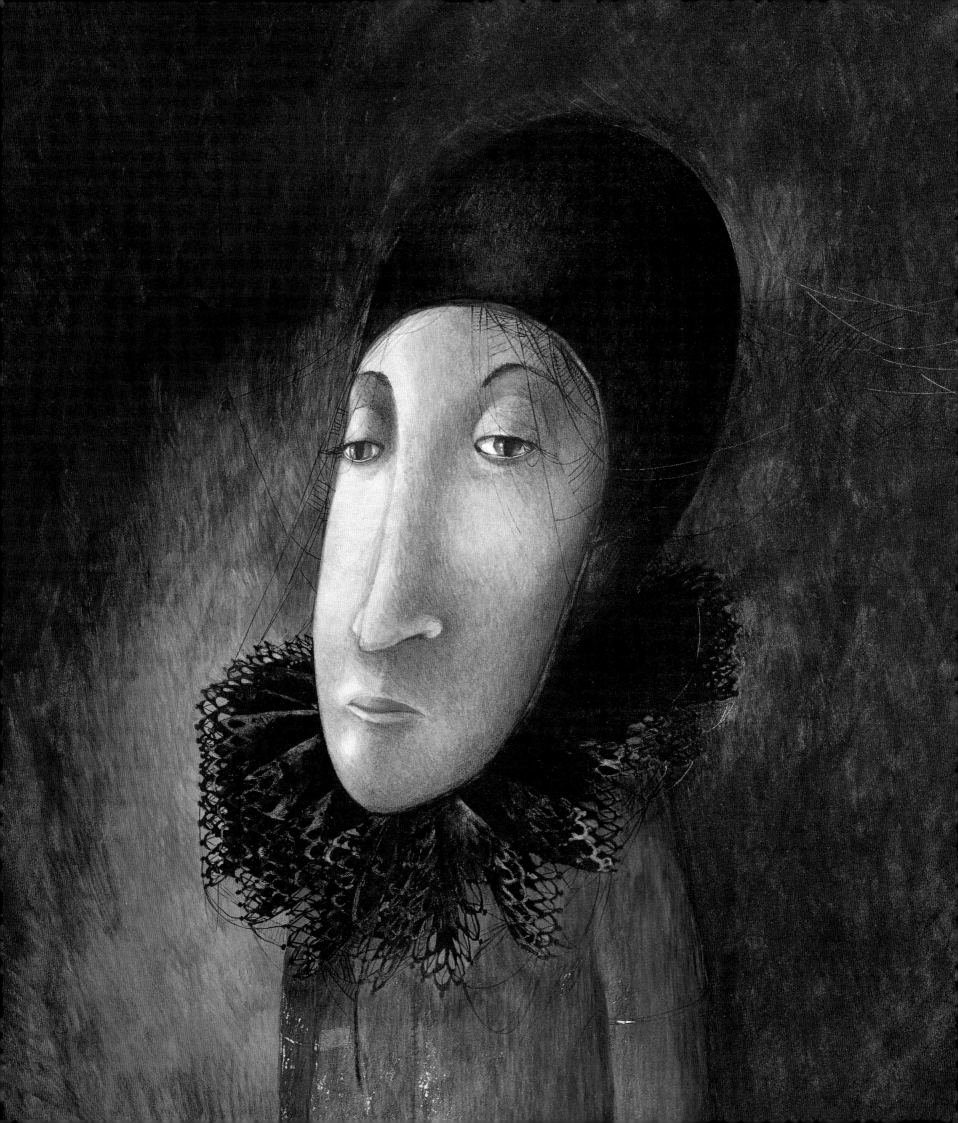

Princess Sticky-Fingers

No locks, no bolts, no doors can block the conniving Princess Sticky-Fingers.

She slips in everywhere, cracks safes with great style, and leaves without a trace. During fancy balls, she relieves other princesses of their rings and necklaces simply by walking close to them. And while dancing, she steals the wallets of counts, princes, and barons.

Always masked. Never caught.

Avoid her if you see her.

Princess Zig-Zag

Faster than the speed of light. Elusive.

Impossible to control. Never stops.

JEWELS:

Bangles, bracelets, necklaces, earrings . . . princesses adore wearing mounds of jewelry. Among their many treasures, they are particularly fond of rings set with precious stones.

Princesses believe that certain stones hold miraculous powers. The moonstone is their favorite: They claim that it cures hiccups, banishes all evil thoughts, and prevents bad grades in math. The aquamarine also is very popular: It helps lazy princesses get out of bed and allows restless ones to fall asleep.

The ruby heals dizziness, and the diamond helps avoid the brushing of teeth. The amethyst lets you climb steep mountains, and the emerald helps you descend them.

As for amber, some people say that it helps attract princes, while others believe it makes them flee. It is not an exact science, however. If you listen to the experts, you may find this is all a little bit of this and a little of that, a whole lot of blah blah blah, and a smattering of goobledygook.

The future is a story whose plot is unknown.

Princess Claire Voyant

Princess Claire Voyant is very, very small,

much smaller than most of her friends.

But she can see very, very far, even into tomorrow.

On Monday she has visions of what will happen Tuesday, on Wednesday she looks well into Thursday,

and so on until Sunday.

On Sunday she rests.

She reads tarot cards, tea leaves, palms, even the feet of spiders.

The problem is this: She is usually wrong.

She gets the days muddled in her predictions, mixes up first names and last, and confuses clubs with spades,

hearts with diamonds. She is frequently bewildered and consequently not very much in demand.

CRYSTAL BALL:
Full of light and full of lies.
Believe at your own risk.

CARDS:
In card games, you can find kings, queens, jacks,
and sometimes jesters. But not one princess.
This is simply unacceptable.
Refuse to play card games which don't include
princesses.
Boycott the king of spades, the queen of diamonds,
and the jack of clubs.
Always keep an extra princess of hearts with you.

Secrets may be locked away, but they dream of escaping.

A Confidante

A confidante, or closest friend, accompanies a princess at all times.

She advises, corrects, and consoles.

Soul sister, kindred spirit, or BFF, she shares life's most intense moments as well as the boring ones. She holds the princess's hand when she is sad, stands by her side no matter what happens, and is her shoulder to lean on in case of a hard blow.

She is in on all the princess's private thoughts, mysteries, and intrigues.

More than a simple companion, the confidante is

a locked safe that keeps all the princess's secrets.

There are many stories of great friendships between a princess and her confidante. Some last only a short time, like those of Princess For-a-Day. (see page 58)

Then there are exceptions like the Flip-Flop sisters. They don't need confidantes, as they never leave each other's side. They have no choice but to share their secrets with each other. (see page 52)

The Unknown Princess

No one knows who she is. It is impossible to find the tiniest clue about her.

However, she exists.

Write to me if you have any information.

SECRETS:
The world of princesses is full of secrets. Princesses have secret plans, secret staircases, secret drawers, and secret treasure chests. Their doors are locked and their thoughts concealed. However, sometimes secrets are revealed as if carried in by a mysterious breeze. Other secrets are never discovered.

KEY:
Used to open doors, safes, and locked journals. Several models are available: the heavy and celebrated golden key for the castle doors of well-to-do princesses; the key to the hidden forest, for the princess who likes to frolic in the outdoors; and also the famous slumber key, which reveals the secret meaning of dreams.

Princess Oblivia

She misses all appointments, never catches the train on time, and arrives at the theater either one week early or three days late.

She forgets everything:

who she is, who you are, what she's going to do, and why you are there.

She has no memory, only a big black hole in its place.

IS RELATED TO:

Cinderella

Was so absentminded that she completely forgot that her carriage would transform into a pumpkin and her dress into rags when the clock struck midnight.

Princess of the Disorient

Is completely out of the ordinary.

Her kingdom fits her image: wacky,

filled with fools,

and complete with nutty celebrations.

Nothing is straightforward. Everything is haywire, mixed up, and backwards. Parents do homework and children watch television late into the night. Boys wear dresses and girls sport beards. Dogs walk their masters on leashes.

In her kingdom, the beautiful are ugly and the ugly are beautiful. To lie is to speak the truth.

The Princess of the Disorient was married by accident to King Loopdilou.

Princess Amorphia

As her name indicates,

Princess Amorphia

is a bit of a mystery.

Upside-down,

downside-up.

A work in progress.

ATTENTION

Don't forget to remind yourself to think about remembering

Prince S.

"Do you want to switch places?" a princess asked her look-alike brother one day. "Sure," he responded. "The first one to give in loses."
So the prince passed himself off as the princess
  and vice versa.
The swap went undiscovered for some time, until the prince's voice became deeper, he began to grow a beard, and not a single dress fit him.
But he refused to give in and lose the contest. He went to the best tailor in the kingdom and had new dresses custom-made. He braided his beard and moustache.
The competition continues to this day.
The members of the court are too polite to point out the princess's strange look.
She is known as Prince S.

Paris. 10. VII. 04

Princess Quartermoon

Fourth daughter of Full Moon and Lonely Bear.

Lives in the Great Plains, where you can hear the coyote's cry and the eagle's song. Wears a regal cloak woven from thousands of beads.

Spends hours sending smoke signals to her friends, which drives her parents crazy. Creates special totems—sacred items or symbols that make wishes come true.

TOTEMS:

It's not difficult to use totems, but precautions must be taken to avoid mishaps.

To make rain fall:
Take a fistful of dirt in your left hand and perform three complete turns in one direction, and seven in the other. Then wait. (Don't forget your umbrella.)

To make the sun come out:
Take six turns to the right, and twelve to the left. Repeat until the sun appears. Then wait. (Wear comfy shoes.)

To make a wish come true:
Do the same thing as for the sun but hop on one foot. Then wait. (Allow for lots of time.)

To have fun:
Spin around anytime, anyplace, and anywhere. Don't wait to repeat. (Bring lots of good friends.)

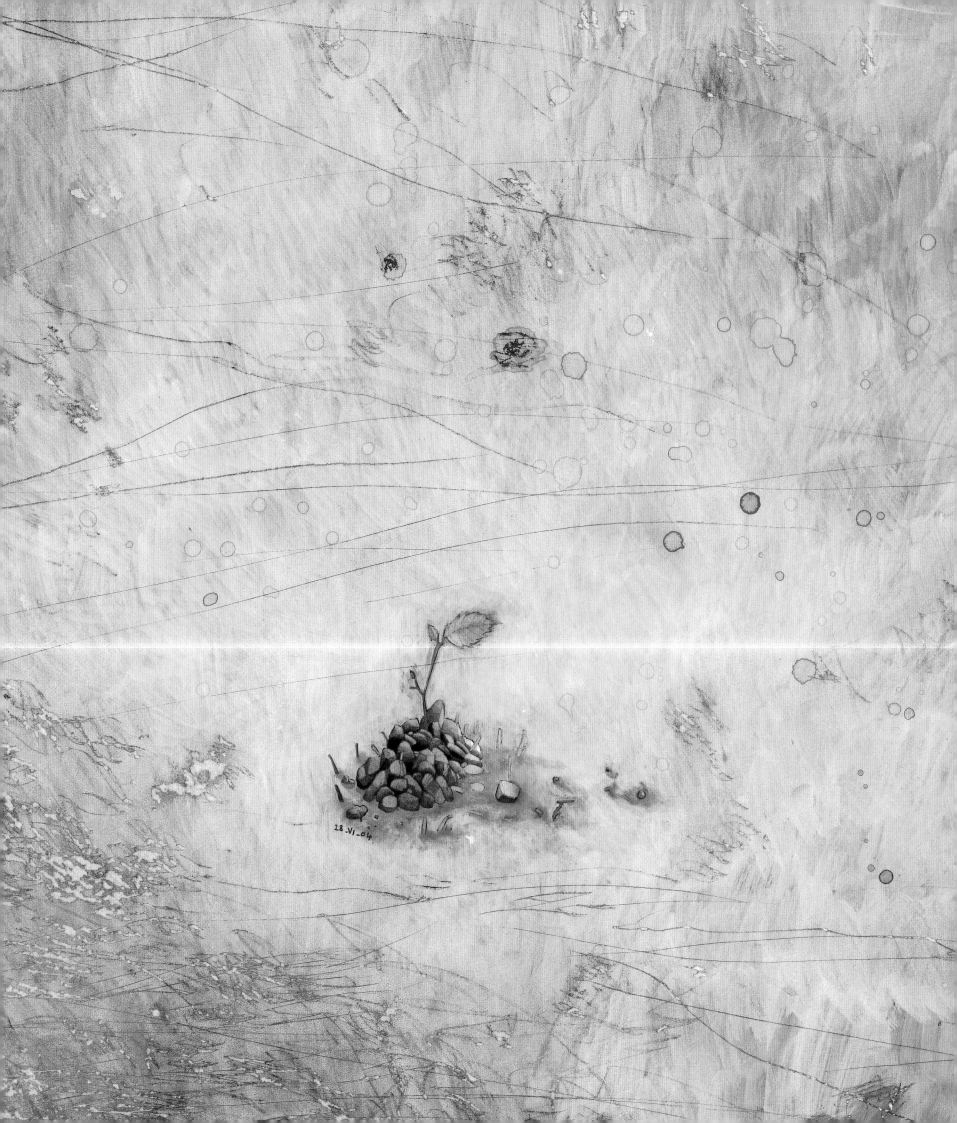

28-VI-04

COATS OF ARMS AND FLAGS

Princess Picaresque's unicycle

Claire Voyant's life-line

Amorphia's spare parts

Oblivia's memory
(not to be confused with the Princess of the Disorient's square)

Princess Ices's favorite snack

The faceless Princess's fake mustache

Site of Hot-Head's famous victory

Meetu's plume

Anne Phibian's net

Prince S.'s razor

Flip and Flop's double-clapper bell

The Princess of the Disorient's square

Primandproper's wasp
Do-Re-Mi's violin holes

Alli fabette's thinking cap

Zig-Zag's spring
(not to be confused with the Princess Tangra-la's party streamer)

Somnia's cushion

BE QUIET—I'M SLEEPING

Babbling Brooke's megaphone

Fa-Sol-La's throat

Miss Hap's piece of duct tape

The Eco Princess's dog toy

Tangra-la's party streamer

Paige's glasses

The Night Princess's gloom

Sticky-Fingers's keyhole

Molly Coddle's eyelash comb

The Invisible Princess's . . .

Barbara of Babel's tongue

For-a-Day's stopwatch

Quartermoon's full moon

Princess Eelizabeth's air bubble (not to be confused with the Princess of the Disorient's square)

The Princess of the Sands's shovel and rake

Thimbelina's bonbon
(not to be confused with Princess Somnia's cushion)

The Fingerprint of the Unknown Princess

43

Voyages

Whether walking, by train, on a donkey, or the back of an eagle, princesses love to travel the world.

For many princesses, traveling by elephant provides a change of scenery.

But it can be **rather uncomfortable,**

so it's best to set up **a little palace on its back**

with a bathtub and a built-in balcony

so the princess can salute the crowds.

Ancient princesses used elephants to help them plant flowers in the famous gardens of Babylon, one of the seven wonders of the ancient world. Their trunks were very useful for morning showers and for watering the plants.

Princess Molly Coddle has a train with three bathrooms, while Princess Miss Hap uses a zeppelin built in order to escape from the island where she had been exiled.

(see Princess Molly Coddle, page 22, and Princess Miss Hap, page 24)

a. *exit*
b. *porch swing*
c. *herb garden*
d. *clothes lines*
e. *dining room*
f. *hammock for naps (in the shade)*
g. *baggage*
h. *retractable stairs*
i. *balcony (where a princess can greet her public)*
j. *study*
k. *bedroom*
l. *garden tools and snow shovel*
m. *wastewater*
n. *tennis court*
o. *outdoor shower*
p. *hidden passageway*
q. *main water valve*
r. *doorbell (pull hard)*
s. *Bernard (the driver)*

Princess Barbara of Babel

Speaks a multitude of languages. All the time.

Her first language, foreign languages,

living languages, dead languages,

and even sign language.

Currently conversant in French, English, Farsi, and Chinese. Also practices Arabic, Swahili, Hungarian, and, it goes without saying, Javanese. She writes a little in Latin and Alsatian. She has some grasp of Italian and Korean, and writes poetry in Mongolian without difficulty. She is well-versed in the slang of Texas and Azerbaijan. She knows every Russian verb, Bulgarian adjective, and Lithuanian pronoun.

Practiced in high diplomatic functions, she is the royal ambassador of all the courts' princesses.

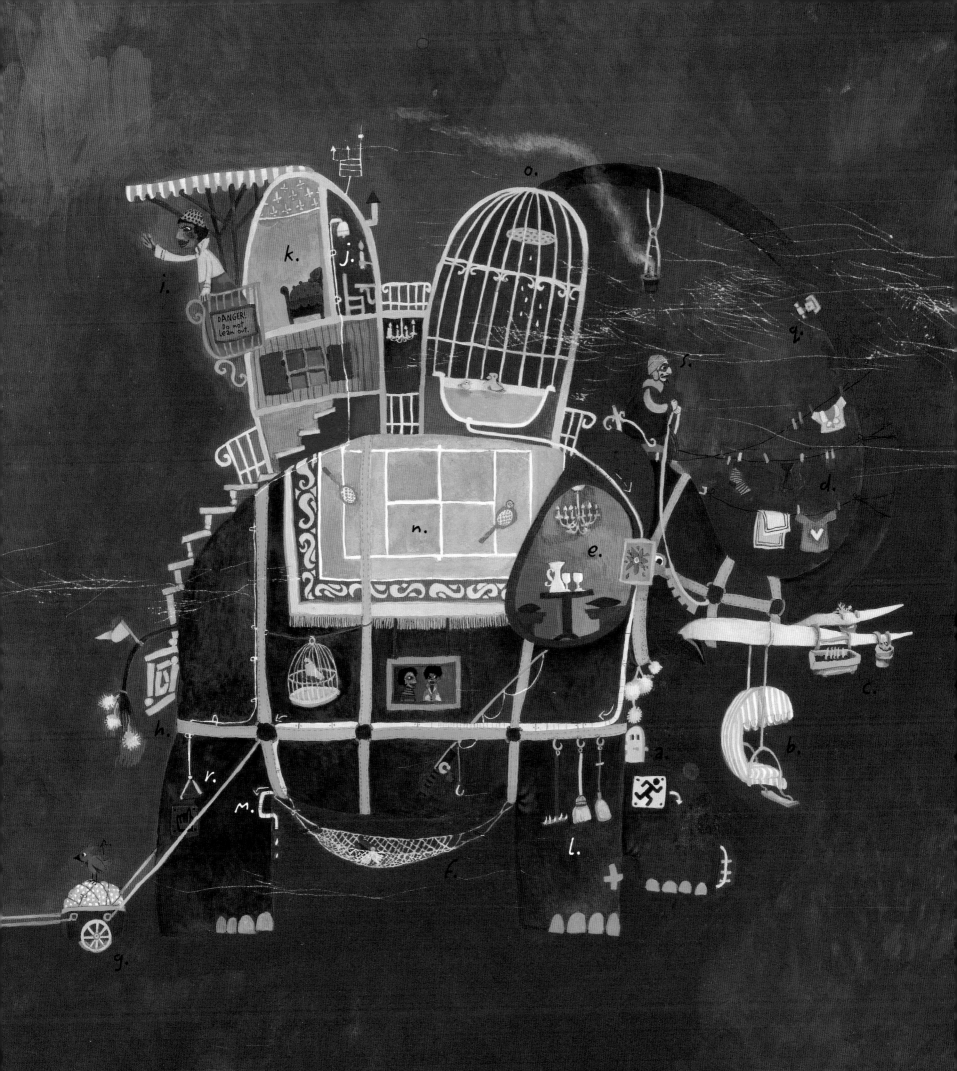

You have to take your feet off the ground if you're going to reach the sky.

Princess Picaresque

Princess Picaresque is a princess unlike all the others.

Her palace is a caravan drawn by a horse. Her kingdom knows no boundaries. She has already circled the earth several times, getting by with her sharp wits.

Her father does not wear a crown. His teeth are made of gold, and that is his only treasure. Princess Picaresque is a circus artist. Accompanied by all her court, she travels from town to town to perform grand feats of daring and awe. Her favorite trick is to walk a tightrope so high it cuts through the clouds.

A tree is a
house full of
possibilities.

The Eco Princess

The court of the Eco Princess is made up of amazing subjects:

snakes, zebras, tigers, cheetahs, and panthers.

She is at home in all parts of nature—jungles, savannahs, rainforests . . . She ties up her

beautiful hair with vines from trees. It is a very elegant look.

Birds nest in her gorgeous hair and whisper secrets to her
of princesses of long ago.

She spends her evenings chatting in her tree palace with her closest confidantes and animal

protectors. She will only accept a prince who is not afraid of heights, lightning, or beetles.

One day I found the veil of a distant princess in my garden.

The Princess of the Sands

Daughter of the Queen of Saba, this princess lives in a castle of sand whose location depends on the direction of the winds.

It shifts to the north

when the sirocco blows

hot and dry.

To the south during

the season of the simoom.

To the west

when the harmattan rages.

And to the east

the rest of the time.

She bathes in oases,

knows the names of every stone and star,

and wears a veil as protection from the storms.

She grows desert roses.

VEIL:

From a very young age, princesses practice walking around their palaces, wearing long veils trailing behind them. These elegant accessories are so linked with some princesses, it's as if they were born with them. Whether transparent or opaque, embroidered with gold thread or made of simple cotton, the veil can reveal details about the princess, while still keeping her most precious secrets inside. A linen veil indicates a princess from the countryside. Heavy wool protects those who live in stone palaces in the mountains. And for the fashion-forward city-dwelling princess, the trend this season is for a short veil in the sheerest organdy.

Make a veil that reveals **YOUR TRUE SELF**
All you need is scissors and style!

Princesses Flip and Flop

Princesses of the kingdom of Siam, they are famous throughout the East.

These twins are inseparable. Literally.

They wear the same kimono

and share one pair of sandals.

They live in a palace made for two and wake up to the sound of silver-tipped hooves clattering as their carriage comes to fetch them each morning.

Their favorite hobbies are telling knock-knock jokes and playing croquet.

Descendants of the famous princess cousins Sing and Song.

Princess Hot-Head

Has the face of an angel, but behaves like a devil.

Totally terrifying.

Prefers brandishing a sword to practicing the piano,

chooses horse races over needlepoint.

Can't tolerate complaining.

Runs faster than everyone, spits on the ground, and challenges

everyone to arm-wrestling matches.

Wounded during the battle of Atalanta.

Friend of Amazons.

Her big secret? She's afraid of mice. (see Mini Tree Mouse, page 63)

CAT-O'-NINE-TAILS:
Horrible device made with multiple rawhide whips.
Very dangerous.

AMAZONS:
Princesses who hate princes. Feast on steak tartare and train themselves to handle the Cat-O'-Nine-Tails
(see above). Peerless horsewomen, they even sleep on their steeds. They frighten everyone and fear no
one, not even the ogre, Offal the Awful. (see *Royal Cuisine or How to Prepare a Princess: Twenty Simple and
Savory Recipes*, page 79)

Pocket
Cat-O'-Nine-Tails

Portable!
Great for vacations!

P.H.H.

Uses 6 AAA batteries
(sold separately)

Tested and Approved
by Princess Hot-Head

Travel-size

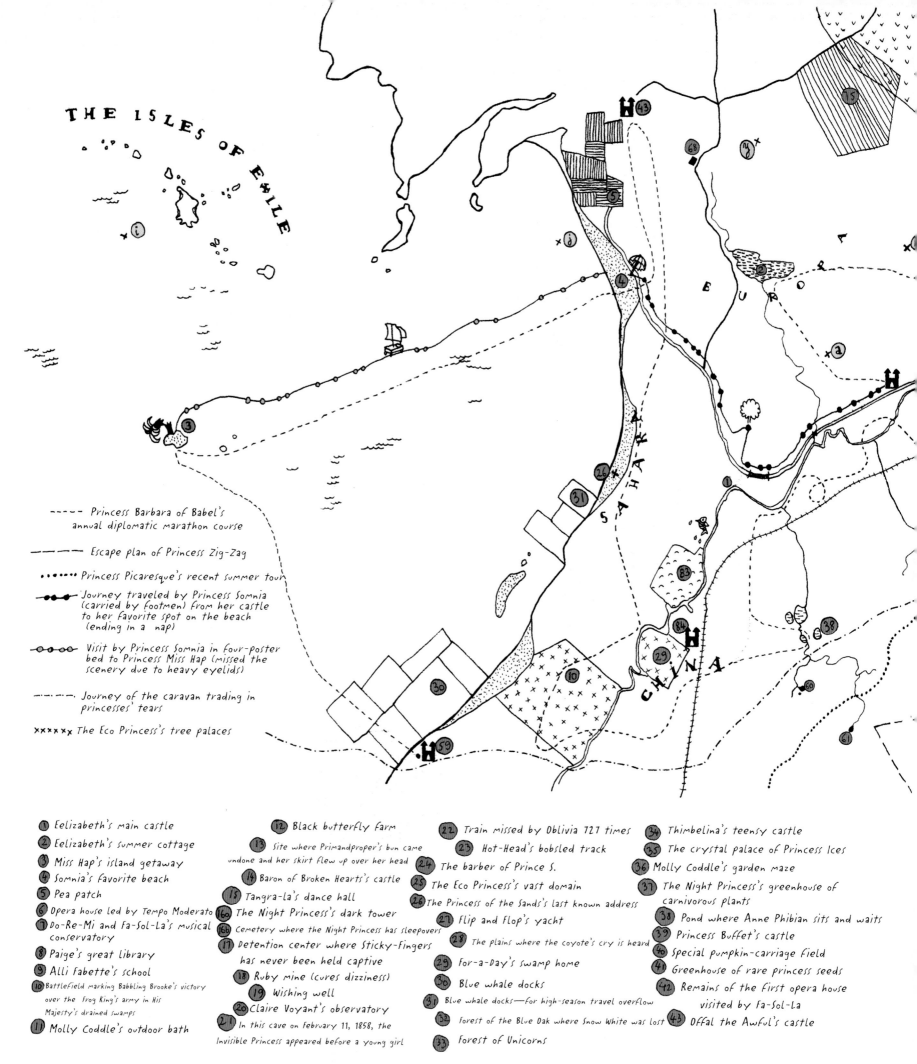

THE ISLES OF EXILE

---- Princess Barbara of Babel's annual diplomatic marathon course

— Escape plan of Princess Zig-Zag

••••• Princess Picaresque's recent summer tour

●━●━ Journey traveled by Princess Somnia (carried by footmen) from her castle to her favorite spot on the beach (ending in a nap)

◉━◉━ Visit by Princess Somnia in four-poster bed to Princess Miss Hap (missed the scenery due to heavy eyelids)

—·—· Journey of the caravan trading in princesses' tears

×××××× The Eco Princess's tree palaces

1 Eelizabeth's main castle
2 Eelizabeth's summer cottage
3 Miss Hap's island getaway
4 Somnia's favorite beach
5 Pea patch
6 Opera house led by Tempo Moderato
7 Do-Re-Mi and Fa-Sol-La's musical conservatory
8 Paige's great library
9 Alli fabette's school
10 Battlefield marking Babbling Brooke's victory over the frog King's army in His Majesty's drained swamps
11 Molly Coddle's outdoor bath

12 Black butterfly farm
13 Site where Primandproper's bun came undone and her skirt flew up over her head
14 Baron of Broken Hearts's castle
15 Tangra-la's dance hall
16a The Night Princess's dark tower
16b Cemetery where the Night Princess has sleepovers
17 Detention center where Sticky-fingers has never been held captive
18 Ruby mine (cures dizziness)
19 Wishing well
20 Claire Voyant's observatory
21 In this cave on February 11, 1858, the Invisible Princess appeared before a young girl

22 Train missed by Oblivia 727 times
23 Hot-Head's bobsled track
24 The barber of Prince S.
25 The Eco Princess's vast domain
26 The Princess of the Sands's last known address
27 Flip and Flop's yacht
28 The plains where the coyote's cry is heard
29 For-a-Day's swamp home
30 Blue whale docks
31 Blue whale docks—for high-season travel overflow
32 Forest of the Blue Oak where Snow White was lost
33 Forest of Unicorns

34 Thimbelina's teensy castle
35 The crystal palace of Princess Ices
36 Molly Coddle's garden maze
37 The Night Princess's greenhouse of carnivorous plants
38 Pond where Anne Phibian sits and waits
39 Princess Buffet's castle
40 Special pumpkin-carriage field
41 Greenhouse of rare princess seeds
42 Remains of the first opera house visited by Fa-Sol-La
43 Offal the Awful's castle

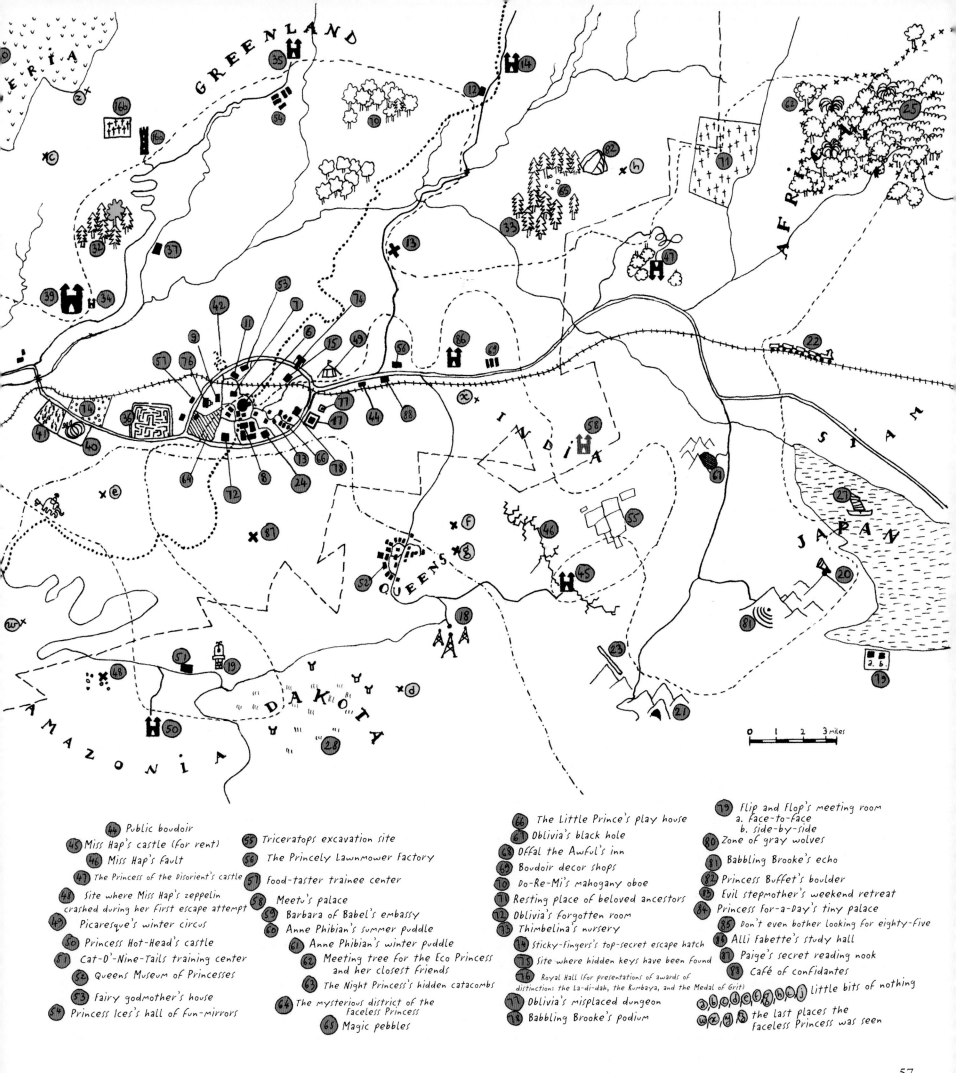

Public boudoir
Miss Hap's castle (for rent)
Miss Hap's fault
The Princess of the Disorient's castle
Site where Miss Hap's zeppelin crashed during her first escape attempt
Picaresque's winter circus
Princess Hot-Head's castle
Cat-O'-Nine-Tails training center
Queens Museum of Princesses
Fairy godmother's house
Princess Ices's hall of fun-mirrors

Triceratops excavation site
The Princely Lawnmower Factory
Food-taster trainee center
Meetu's palace
Barbara of Babel's embassy
Anne Phibian's summer puddle
Anne Phibian's winter puddle
Meeting tree for the Eco Princess and her closest friends
The Night Princess's hidden catacombs
The mysterious district of the faceless Princess
Magic pebbles

The Little Prince's play house
Oblivia's black hole
Offal the Awful's inn
Boudoir decor shops
Do-Re-Mi's mahogany oboe
Resting place of beloved ancestors
Oblivia's forgotten room
Thimbelina's nursery
Sticky-fingers's top-secret escape hatch
Site where hidden keys have been found
Royal Hall (for presentations of awards of distinction: the La-di-dah, the Kumbaya, and the Medal of Grit)
Oblivia's misplaced dungeon
Babbling Brooke's podium

Flip and Flop's meeting room
a. face-to-face
b. side-by-side
Zone of gray wolves
Babbling Brooke's echo
Princess Buffet's boulder
Evil stepmother's weekend retreat
Princess For-a-Day's tiny palace
Don't even bother looking for eighty-five
Alli fabette's study hall
Paige's secret reading nook
Café of confidantes
little bits of nothing
the last places the faceless Princess was seen

57

Princess For-a-Day

A member of a special and mysterious dynasty where a princess exists for only one day.

She is very pretty, as graceful as a dragonfly,

and as light as air.

LIFE CYCLE:

The life of Princess For-a-Day only lasts a few hours: In the morning, she wakes up in her cocoon. Then she grows up very quickly until she's ready to fly with her own wings. You can spot her in gardens, dressed in magnificent robes and breathing in the perfume of flowers. She swirls and twirls under a brilliant sun, listening to the flattery of the heavily armored princes who make up her court. Then the evening arrives and her reign is over. With a fluttering of wings, she disappears in the night, illuminated by fireflies.

HABITAT:

China, but also North Africa and Europe in the summer months. Sometimes found on sunlit prairies if the temperature is between 89 and 91 degrees Fahrenheit.

CLASSIFICATION:

The reign of Dame Diaphanous, Princess For-a-Day the 337th:

August 6, 2009, from 5:52 a.m. to 11:37 p.m.

Daughter of Queen Quantifly III, granddaughter of Nana Nanosec.

Brief yet loyal friend to many (see A Confidante, page 34)

Nana Nanosec
(August 4, 2009, 4:38 a.m. to 7:11 p.m.)

Queen Quantifly III
(August 5, 2009, 6:50 a.m. to 8:18 p.m.)

Dame Diaphanous
(August 6, 2009, 5:52 a.m. to 11:37 p.m.)

Chrysalis the Sylph
(August 7, 2009, 9:01 a.m. to 11:35 p.m.)

Queen Quantifly IV, nicknamed
"The Small"
(August 8, 2009,
10:10 a.m. to 9 p.m.)

Ephemeral Flitter
(August 9, 2009, 8:29 a.m. to 9:17 p.m.)

Lucentia the Eternal
(August 10, 2009, 3:04 a.m. to
11:37 p.m.)

Madame Meteor
(August 11, 2009, 4:13 a.m. to 9:39 p.m.)
Sprightly the Magnificent
(August 12, 2009, 6:22 a.m. to 9:37 p.m.)
The Duchess of Gauzy
(August 13, 2009, 5:49 a.m. to 9:39 p.m.)
Gossamer the Great
(August 14, 2009, 4:31 a.m. to 9:40 p.m.)
Princess Alacrity
(August 15, 2009, 5:01 a.m. to 9:36 p.m.)

Live in the sunshine, swim the sea, drink the wild air.

Princess Eelizabeth

It is very hard to spot
Princess Eelizabeth.
She only comes up for air once a year,
when she meets up with her prince charming, Baron Triton.
A stylish swimmer, she slips through the river depths and glides
under ice-covered streams.
If you are very patient, you might catch a glimpse of her white skin,
slightly bluish, almost silvery, along the pebbly river bottom.
She is always ready to fight bravely through the watery torrents or swim
against the current.

Is the daughter of Delta Smelt,
principal admiral of the royal navy,
and the sister of the wriggling princesses Alba Core and Anne Chovy.

60

BLACK BUTTERFLY:

A black butterfly forecasts doom, just like a pirate flag.

Once you see one, there's little hope.

(see Princess Primandproper, page 26)

GRAY WOLF:

A legend recounts that a wandering princess was adopted by a pack of gray wolves. They took care of her and she grew up surrounded by their affection. Legend says she lives in Siberia and that an old gray wolf is always by her side. Some say the pack can be heard at night when the wind blows.

INSEPARABLE LOVEBIRDS:

These two birds accompany the Princesses Flip and Flop wherever they go. Completely identical in every respect, they resemble each other like two drops of water: Flip's bird is called King and Flop's is called Kong.

Remember that now:

King belongs to Flip and Kong belongs to Flop.

But sometimes King is with Flop

and Kong is with Flip.

(see Princesses Flip and Flop, page 52)

BLUE WHALE:

The preferred means of transportation for

princesses who cannot stand the discomfort

of traveling on elephant back.

(see Voyages, pages 44 and 45)

More spacious and dignified than the grandest

cruise ships.

Crossing the Atlantic Ocean via Reykjavik is a particularly

popular route nowadays.

Consider reserving a seat ahead of time.

UNICORN:

A type of horse with a twisted horn on its forehead. A favorite animal of princesses everywhere. Notable for its surpassing beauty and extreme sensitivity. Has the distinction of being seen only by princesses. In order to meet a unicorn, several precautions must be taken: You have to wear your most beautiful dress before entering the forest. Then sit on a hollow log and wait. When the unicorn emerges, it will approach, place its head on your knees, and fall asleep. Over the years, the unicorns have shared their cares and concerns with princesses. All these confidences were gathered together in a book, *A Unicorn's Tail and Other Magical Stories*, but it's now sadly out of print and impossible to find. But if you're very lucky, you might uncover a mislaid copy hidden somewhere in an attic, in a cupboard, or at the back of a very old and dusty bookstore.

PARANORMAL TARANTULA:

Used by princesses since the beginning of time to see the future. Its footpads are dipped in ink and then one tries to decipher the message it leaves on a large sheet of paper. If you don't have a tarantula on hand (or if you are really scared of spiders), you can also use large flies. It's the same process, but the marks they leave are smaller and much harder to read.

(see Princess Claire Voyant, page 32)

MINI TREE MOUSE:

Princess Hot-Head isn't afraid of anything. She is ready to confront all dangers: a dragon, a horde of barbarous villains, an attack of iguanodons. The only thing that bothers her is the very cute mini tree mouse.

(see Princess Hot-Head, page 54)

PINK RHINOCEROS:

The pink rhinoceros is ideal for children. A lot less frightening than the gray or white rhinoceros, and much better smelling. Completely gentle, one was given to Princess Thimbelina as a companion and proved to be the only creature who could calm her sometimes silly moods.

(see Princess Thimbelina, page 66)

COCO DODO:

A fabulous bird with a fiery plumage. A favorite of princesses, their feathers are occasionally found on their gowns and hats. Very rare.

Forest

Forests provide great places of refuge for princesses.

They can get lost there,

seek comfort,

hide,

or have extraordinary adventures.

The forest is home to a multitude of creatures:

dwarves (generally in groups of seven), ogres, goblins,

lost princes, dragons, sorcerers, and unicorns.

(see Unicorn, page 63)

Some forests are deep

and dark,

full of thorny shrubs, wild boars,

and poisonous mushrooms.

The trees all begin to look alike and the muddy paths

merge and disappear before you even realize it.

In the middle of winter, you can hear the cries of

hungry wolves.

Other forests

are full of light,

home to birds, deer, hares, and other animals with

gentle, shiny eyes. Clear springs run through them and

the sun pierces the canopy of leaves. You can gather

berries and fall asleep on a lazy afternoon.

And then there is the forest

whose name is long forgotten.

This is where, sometimes on a Sunday walk off the

beaten path, you might see the fabled blue oak.

A forest holds many secrets.

BLUE OAK:
Extremely rare, the blue oak is a protected species. Recognizable by its aroma of fresh mint and cut herbs, it can be found at the edge of a trail or at the bottom of a ravine. If you spot one, watch carefully: A princess is usually close by.

STONES:

All princesses possess at least one special stone. Each one is very different: gathered on a beach, from a grotto, or on a dirt path; made of mica, of limestone, in red, gray, or green; rough or polished smooth; lucky or filled with evil spells; hidden in a pocket, gripped in a fist, or even enclosed in a secret cupboard. No princess would ever show you her stone. It's useless to insist; it's a secret charm never to be revealed.

(see Secrets, page 34)

The only exception is Princess Buffet and her giant boulder, where she likes to host picnics.

(see Princess Buffet, page 80)

Tiny and sweet, but with a bite.

Princess Thimbelina

Little Prince

The princess's younger brother.

1. Small. Much, much smaller than the majority of princesses. Has, however, an unfortunate tendency to see himself as much, much larger,

   generally as the biggest prince around.

2. A dreamer, lost in the stars, living on a cloud accompanied by several servants.

Occasional nicknames: small fry, shrimp.

She's just a little bit of a thing.

A cutie patootie.

A gem and a jewel not much bigger than your thumb.

She's a real sweetie,

but can sometimes get a little silly,

mostly at night.

The only solution, a lullaby sung by a pink rhinoceros, which sets everything right.

(see page 63)

BABY TEETH:
Preserved with great care in a chest locked with a key (see Key, page 34) to prevent mice from carrying them away.
Thimbelina's baby teeth, the smallest ever known, are on display at the Queens Museum of Princesses.
Go visit them when you can.

Paris — 10 04 04

The Queen

How do you become a queen?

For many princesses, this occurs at the time of their marriage:

a princess becomes a queen,

which offers a certain number of advantages,

like the right to wear make-up without being scolded.

However, some remain princesses all their life. There is one who is

more than ninety-seven years old, still agile, still graceful.

STEPMOTHER:
Occasional replacement for the queen, due to
unforeseen and unfortunate circumstances.
While most are full of love, a rare few can be very
disagreeable, not to say unbearable, not to say
downright detestable (Cinderella's stepmother was a
fine example of this type). These stepmothers even
complain about the size of their palaces.
The evil kind of stepmother can't bear to see her
stepdaughter wearing a prettier dress than hers.
She can't stand it if her stepdaughter is more
beautiful than she is.
She flaunts her crocodile handbags and false
eyelashes.
This kind of stepmother usually wears too much
perfume.

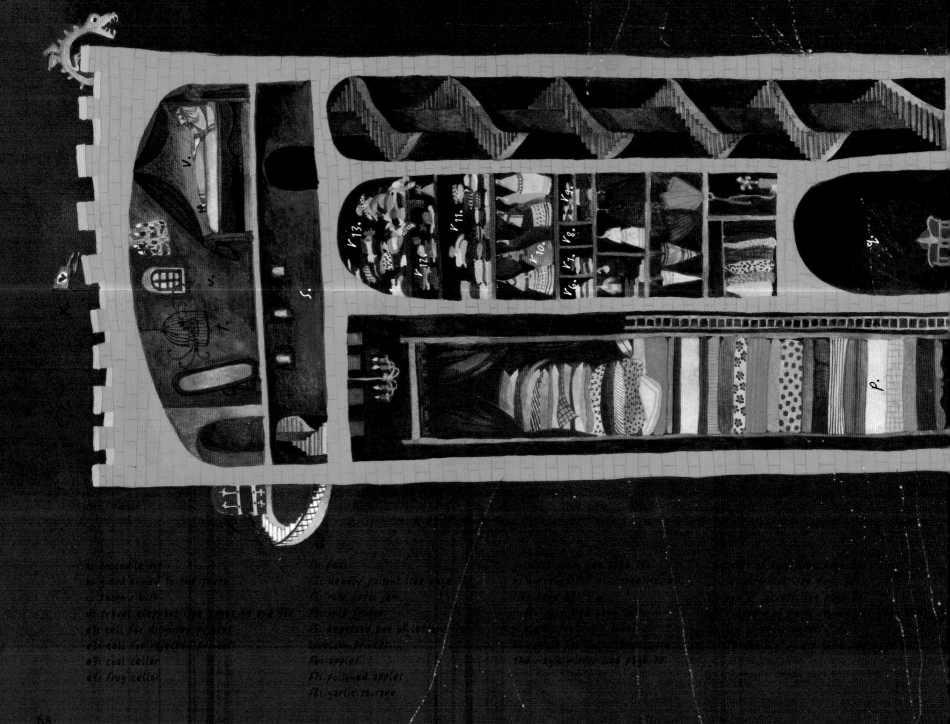

TOWER:

Any self-respecting castle or palace includes a tower perched at the very top of the structure. That's where you can generally find the princess's bedroom, often at the end of a long staircase and a rather dark corridor. The princess's tower is usually decorated quite tastefully.

• As you would expect, Princess Meetu's tower is the most original, with self-portraits hung on the walls. (see Princess Meetu, page 82)

• Princess Ices's tower is completely transparent, made of crystal with stalactite curtains. It's very pretty, but not terribly practical. (see Princess Ices, page 70)

• Everything in Princess Miss Hap's tower is broken, and you can find nothing in Princess Oblivia's. (see Princess Miss Hap, page 24, and Princess Oblivia, page 36)

• As for the tower of the Unknown Princess, no one has ever seen it. (see The Unknown Princess, page 34)

Princes are quite knowledgeable about tower rooms and know that they are difficult to enter. Anyone who tries to climb up faces dragons, extraordinary height, armed guards, and crocodile pits. There was one quite ingenious princess who unbraided her long hair so that a prince could climb it and reach her room. Unfortunately for the prince, a witch cut the hair with a pair of scissors when he was almost at the top and he landed in a thorny bush. (see Princess, page 76)

Princess Ices

The Snow Queen's great-granddaughter. Lives by herself in an immense palace of crystal and ice. Reopened the mirror factory founded by her great-grandmother, who invented a mirror that proved to be a commercial failure: Composed entirely of frost, it transformed the beautiful into the ugly.

Princess Ices revitalized the business by offering new products:

- A fun-house mirror

- A mirror that allows you to watch TV while brushing your hair

- An entire range of brooding mirrors, for when you feel the most sad, hopeless, or pathetic

- A vanity mirror. Used by Snow White's stepmother. Comes with voice recognition and access code. Generally begins with "Mirror, mirror on the wall, who's the fairest of them all?"

- A vice versa mirror (very similar to Alice's looking-glass). Simply step through it as you would enter a doorway and find yourself in another world. Aware that people often live in homes that are smaller than palaces, Princess Ices made it the company's key product. The marketing slogan:

The vice versa mirror!
You don't need to leave home
to leave home.

PALACES AND RESIDENCES

basic model

basic model with options
(balcony, front steps, four towers,
and terrace with cherubs)

rescue tower

hidden

rustic

inuit

moroccan

multi-family

parisian

pompeii

lilliputian

coastal

gothic

manhattan walk-up

las vegas

portable

french provincial

egyptian

RV

The Garden

An extraordinary garden, an English garden, or a French garden,

all princesses possess at least a little corner of green.

The poorest princesses sneak their flowers into hidden patches where no one knows.

It is their secret garden.

The wealthy take long walks around the grounds of their castle.

Their favorite plants: lily and licorice.

Favorite tree: the crowned beechwood.

However, if you are invited, do note that some gardens can be traps. Watch out particularly for the Night Princess's greenhouse of carnivorous plants, as well as Princess Molly Coddle's garden maze. It is whispered that some who have gone in have never come out again.

(see The Night Princess, page 28, and Princess Molly Coddle, page 22)

FLOWERS AND SEEDS:

Each princess has a flower which bears her name.

When you buy seed packets, let the seeds germinate in moist cotton balls and then plant them in your garden or windowsill box. One caution, however: Do not use tap water to water them, only rose nectar.

Some varieties of flowers are easy to cultivate (but still require patience and vigilance):

- The Blue Flower, also called the Thimbelina Weed, is a very tiny yet pretty variety with a colorful bloom and an incomparable aroma. (see Princess Thimbelina, page 66)
- Princess Molly Coddle's Lunatic Narcissus is more fragile but worth trying. Like its namesake, it is a plant which can surprise you. (see Princess Molly Coddle, page 22)
- Princess For-a-Day's Ephemera plant only flourishes briefly, but what a memorable blossom. (see Princess For-a-Day, page 58)
- Princess Somnia's Four-Poster Dandelion needs little maintenance and grows slowly. Perfect for sleepyheads. (see Princess Somnia, page 10)
- Princess Picaresque's Wild Thought grows anywhere. A much less common variety than the Domesticated Thought. (see Princess Picaresque, page 46)
- For an unusual species, try Princess Primandproper's Black Sour. Its bouquet, however, can make you feel ill. (see Princess Primandproper, page 26)
- There is also the rabid nettle called If You Go Looking for Trouble You'll Find It. Not for everyone.

Rose nectar collector

- For the more experienced gardener, the Night Princess's Flower of Evil is a carnivorous flower with dark foliage. Just watch out when you go to bed. (see The Night Princess, page 28)
- And if you have room, try Princess Buffet's Round Rose. (see Princess Buffet, page 80)

PARASOLS:

A wide variety of parasols are available and they make the perfect accessory for strolling in one's garden. The most beautiful and most desirable has golden petals. You can still admire it today in the Queens Museum of Princesses, where it's on display. You can find other models there: the Manila Whirlwind, made of snail shell, as well as a scarlet delight decorated with pearls called the Bangkok Cockle. Other treasures include Princess Meetu's transparent parasol made of a chewing gum bubble (see Princess Meetu, page 82) and the Night Princess's shade, delicately woven from spider webs. (see The Night Princess, page 28)

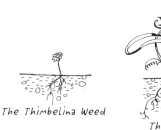

The Thimbelina Weed

The Flower of Evil

The Round Rose

Beneath the stones are flowers not yet born.

Princess Anne Phibian

Search without knowing who he is, but believe that you will recognize him.

Her obsession with frogs is barely evident on the outside.

She's very pretty, doesn't drool, doesn't croak, and doesn't have warts.

Her skin isn't green but rosy pink. She couldn't be sweeter or more refined.

She lives in a palace, not in a pond.

But . . . she is always looking for her Prince Charming and is convinced he is disguised as a frog.

Ever hopeful, she spends most of her time standing in ponds kissing every green creature she encounters.

On last report, she is still soggy and alone.

Her cousin has a similar story but a greater struggle. She believes her prince is hiding in the form of a dinosaur, but it is so difficult to come across a triceratops these days.

Princes

Handsome or ugly,
short or tall,
nasty or nice,
there is an infinite
variety of princes.

Royal lawn mower
(used frequently by married princes)

It is not always easy for a prince to find his princess. He sometimes has to wander through the forest to find the one who is his destiny. Then he has to wake her and kiss her, or kiss her to wake her. Sometimes it ends badly and he's transformed into a frog or some other creature: the common fly, a beetle, or a desert fox. But generally when a prince meets a princess, as the stories say, "they lived happily ever after." But have you noticed that the stories just end there? What really happens to princes after they marry?

KISSES:
There is nothing gentler or sweeter than a princess's kiss.
Quite rare. Should be preserved carefully tucked away in a bottle or in the corner of one's heart.
Light as air, it disappears with the slightest breath.
A princess's kiss has the power to transform frogs into princes, and sometimes the opposite.
Also known as a smooch, a peck, or a big wet one.

Table of TRANSFORMATIONS by type of kiss

Meals

Princesses have a lot of opinions about food.

One princess claimed that she only ate apples. Another said she lunched on rose petal jam every day.

One even declared that all she needed to sustain her were the loving looks from her devoted prince.

(We don't believe these things, but princesses love dramatic stories.)

In fact, princesses eat like everyone else.

The only difference is that everything they swallow

must first be carefully examined

and tested by a taster.

There are always quarrels and scenes going on in the palace, and sometimes these fights are settled

with poison. One can never be too careful.

SORBET:
A light ice cream made of juice and fruit. This is the favorite dessert of princesses. Some of them even eat it as their main course. A wide variety of delicious recipes are available:

Summer sorbet and winter sorbet. Berry sorbet and flower sorbet. The fragrant cardamom sorbet and the cotton candy sorbet, renowned for its lightness.

Breakfast sorbet and midnight snack sorbet. Black sorbet and invisible sorbet.

POISON:
Rancid vinegar, old cheese crusts slipped surreptitiously into a main course, the juice of long-marinated socks, and goose poop are the poisons most commonly used in palace intrigues. Cruel, perhaps, but more effective than pulling someone's hair. Other options:

CHILI:
Tongue heater

PEPPER:
Sneeze dust

SALT:
Guaranteed thirst

Taster

Do you eat everything?

Do you work well with royalty and have a strong stomach?

Proceed immediately to any palace

A pleasant manner is required

Royal Cuisine

or How to Prepare a Princess:
Twenty Simple and Savory Recipes

This famous cookbook was written by Offal the Awful, feared ogre and three-time winner of the Golden Tongue Award.

Specializing in royal dishes,

he only cooks the choicest morsels.

His most famous preparations: Queen Mother's Cake with Royal Icing, Chicken à la King, and Princess Pea Soup.
Ever since his rise to fame, princesses prefer to avoid his restaurant. However, to be personally mentioned in one of his
recipes is considered a significant honor. It speaks of one's great desirability and is a noteworthy (if unsettling) distinction.
But be careful of such flattery. Try to appear in the recipe, but not on the plate.

Even when she was very young, Princess Buffet took up a lot of space. The palaces where she lived and the clothes she wore were always too confining. At school, the other princesses were at first frightened by her unusual size and refused to play hopscotch or other games with her, but they soon realized her size was helpful in defending small kids from bullies and reaching tennis balls from the roof of the school. When she was at home in her palace, she played with the giants.

Later on she married the enormous Prince Brobdingnag, son of the King Gargantua. But their peace only lasted a short time. They both needed so much food to maintain their enormous frames that they bickered regularly over a bit of fat, a roasted pig, or a turkey leg.

Since then, Princess Buffet has spent most of her time planning banquets. Although her size is still off-putting to some, she is generally well-liked and is invited to many parties. She always knows where to find the finest foods to bring, and comes well-stocked with treats. She has been decorated with the prestigious Order of the La-di-dah. (see page 82)

BANQUET:

Princesses plan banquets to celebrate feast days. They compete to see who can be most creative: who will offer the most original dishes and decorate the most festive table. However, no one has yet to surpass the banquet organized by Princess Buffet the day she received the Order of the La-di-dah.

BANQUET MENU:

Lunch:
Vegetable-free salad
12-cheese fondue with purple potatoes
Peanut butter and jam on dragon-toasted bread
Mystery sausage

Snack (a four-hour marathon):
Green lemonade
Magical cupcakes (the plate is never empty)

Dinner:
Pumpkin soup (must be eaten before midnight or it will turn into a carriage)
Rapunzel hair pasta
Luminescent fish soup (you can dim the lights for this course)
Snow White sorbet

The world is your oyster.

To love oneself is the beginning of a life-long romance.

Princess Meetu

The daughter of a maharajah,

and considered one of the most alluring creatures of all time.

She is famous for engaging in numerous scandals,

pushing the boundaries of protocol, upsetting norms, and disregarding convention.

(see Etiquette, page 22)

She wears the most eccentric outfits,

including strange dresses made of paper,

glass, and even plastic.

Her hair is red or sometimes blue,

depending on the day. It is pink when she's in a good mood

and black when she's miserable.

She eats the finest food served to her with her fingers, but uses a knife and fork to carefully

cut french fries.

The interior design of her palace matches her outrageous personality:

zebra-skin sofas, fuchsia-pink flowered walls, orange dishes, and transparent chairs.

She is talked about wherever she goes.

Her only fear: to be ignored. Her only desire: to be adored.

HANDKERCHIEF:
A dainty object which lends itself to a wide variety of uses. Often decorated with pearls or with lace. Every princess has one, although no one can remember ever hearing a princess sneeze. Strange, don't you think?

HOLIDAYS:
Every princess chooses her special holiday, which then becomes a national day off. The Princess of the Disorient decided that every day was a holiday, so no one in her kingdom ever works.

(see page 36)

ENTERTAINMENT:
Provides opportunities to show off a princess's most beautiful dresses, her most unusual veils, and the latest fashions. Very popular activity, whether it's the opera, a concert, the ballet, or a sack race. Most often, the entertainment takes place in the living room. Call ahead to reserve a good seat.

THE ORDER OF THE LA-DI-DAH:
The most prestigious honor which can be bestowed on a princess. Princess Buffet wears her La-di-dah medal with great pride to every banquet.

(see Princess Buffet, page 80)

Another medal, the Kumbaya, is an award of distinction for peaceful conduct.

The Medal of Grit is awarded to those who distinguish themselves in combat.

(see Princess Babbling Brooke, page 18)

PRACTICAL GUIDE
Everything you need to know about princesses

TIPS AND TECHNIQUES TO TELL A TRUE PRINCESS FROM A FAKE ONE

A lot of girls would like to be princesses. Over time, some of them give up their claims and lose their illusions. It is often said that they grow up. (Try to avoid this.) Others, however, pursue their dreams obsessively. They are fixated on becoming princesses and will stop at nothing to achieve their goals. Here are some foolproof ways for recognizing a true princess (and unmasking a fake):

- A true princess never wears socks, not even in the middle of winter.
- A true princess rarely takes off her crown—only when she sleeps, showers, or plays sports.
- Without exception, all princesses sing in the bath.
- A true princess does not bite her nails (at least not in public).
- Princesses are sometimes grumpy.
- Princesses are not always beautiful.
- A true princess does not eat chicken with her fingers (but feet are fine).

TIPS AND TECHNIQUES FOR WAKING A SLEEPING PRINCESS

A kiss seems to be the boldest method and the most successful. Just ask Sleeping Beauty or Snow White. However, some princesses fall into very deep sleeps, which even a kiss from a prince will not break. In these cases, there's only one solution: a bugle.

A bucket of water can also be effective.

Pay extra attention to those who are difficult to wake. If a prince gets the wrong advice, he will suffer the consequences. Just when he has placed a tender kiss on the lips of a sleeping princess, the furious princess will wake up and deliver a punch directly to the chin. No matter what anybody says, a prince's job is often difficult. (see Princes, page 76)

TIPS AND TECHNIQUES FOR SHUSHING A PRINCESS

To this day there is no solution for shushing a princess.

Don't even bother.

EDUCATION AND TRAINING

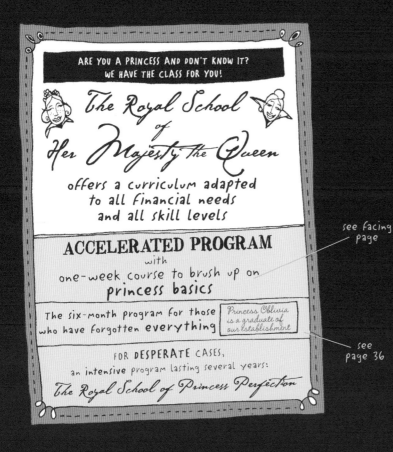

ARE YOU A PRINCESS AND DON'T KNOW IT?
WE HAVE THE CLASS FOR YOU!

The Royal School
of
Her Majesty the Queen

offers a curriculum adapted
to all financial needs
and all skill levels

ACCELERATED PROGRAM
with
one-week course to brush up on
princess basics

The six-month program for those
who have forgotten **everything**

*Princess Oblivia
is a graduate of
our Establishment*

FOR **DESPERATE** CASES,
an intensive program lasting several years:
The Royal School of Princess Perfection

see facing page

see page 36

- WHAT IS MORE FRAGILE THAN A GLASS SLIPPER?
- WHAT COULD BE WORSE THAN SEEING YOUR PRINCE TURN INTO A FROG?
- WHAT IF YOUR PALACE CATCHES FIRE AFTER AN INVASION?
- WHAT IF A PRINCESS SLIPS AND BRUISES HER BOTTOM DURING YOUR BIRTHDAY PARTY?

WHAT A
CATASTROPHE!

TO HANDLE ALL THESE LITTLE CARES AND WOES,
get
Princess Insurance

WE OFFER THE PERFECT POLICY
FOR YOUR PARTICULAR SITUATION.

LESS STRESS, MORE PRINCESS!

- *"I'd be nowhere without my Princess Insurance®."—Princess Miss Hap*
- *"Now with my highness policy from Princess Insurance®, I can chomp on apples with relish."—Snow White*
- *"Princess Insurance®, it's regall."—Princess Alli Fabette*
  carriage no longer turns into

RENTAL AGENCY

To add a touch of glamour and class to an
rent a princess for a day.

When considering a princess to attend your birthd
be sure to choose carefully.

Try to invite Princess Buffet, as she will know whe
the best cake in the kingdom. (see page 80)

Another piece of advice: Avoid Princess Molly Co
a bad loser. (see page 22)

Also note: Some princesses tend to talk talk talk t

(see Tips and Techniques for Shushing a Princess, facing page)

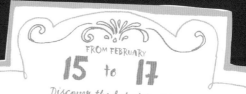

SOS PRINCESS

for princesses in distress, dial
15 15 15 15 15 15 (fairy godmother)
00 00 00 00 00 (text anytime)

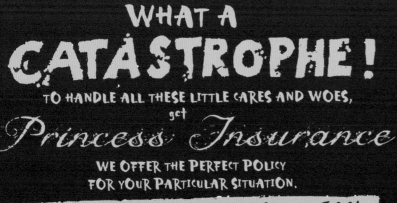

FROM FEBRUARY
15 to 17

Discover the latest fashions
at the
International Festival of Princesses

Royal Salon

MAGIC STONES, NEW STYLES OF SULKING SEATS,
ACCESSORIES (veils, crowns, princes)

PANELS INCLUDE:

*Princes and Princesses: Do They Have a Future?
The Modern Princess: Managing a Career and a Palace
Green Alternatives in Palace Building*

LED BY THE MOST PROMINENT PERSONALITIES
IN THE **WORLD OF PRINCESSES.**

*This year's guests of honor:
Princess Meeta and Princess Tangra-la*

By answering the questions in this test, you can determine what type of princess you are.
Once you have answered all the questions, tally up the total of W, X, Y, and Z responses and discover the real you.
Please note, however, this test is meant only for genuine princesses, those who are searching for themselves, and those who unaware of their true natures.
It is strictly forbidden for fake princesses to take this test. (Management assumes no responsibility for disagreeable transformations.)

1. YOU WERE BORN:
   a. In a rose (W)
   b. In a cabbage (X)
   c. On a bed of sauerkraut (Y)
   d. In the back of a taxi cab (Z)

2. WHEN YOU SEE A FROG:
   a. You kiss it (W)
   b. You eat it (X)
   c. You tame it (Y)
   d. You run away screaming (Z)

3. YOUR FAVORITE FLOWERS ARE:
   a. Dead roses (X)
   b. Dandelions (Z)
   c. Water lilies (Y)
   d. Orchids (W)

4. YOU GREW UP:
   a. In a five-room apartment (Z)
   b. Sheltered (W)
   c. On the run (X)
   d. In a snail shell (Y)

5. COMPLETE THESE LINES OF POETRY:
   "O sad, sad was my soul
   Because, because . . ."
   a. of a palace in flames (X)
   b. of a cold bath (W)
   c. of a poor report card (Z)
   d. of a bellowing stag (Y)

6. YOUR FAVORITE DANCE IS:
   a. The dance of 8,000 tap shoes (Y)
   b. The invisible dance of fans (X)
   c. The glass slipper waltz (W)
   d. You don't dance (Z)

7. WHEN YOU ARE WOKEN BY A PRINCE'S KISS:
   a. You tenderly bat your eyes (W)
   b. You go back to sleep (Y)
   c. You throw him to the crocodiles because he woke you at five in the morning (X)
   d. You have never met a prince (Z)

8. YOUR FAVORITE WEEKEND PASTIME IS:
   a. Braiding unicorn manes (Y)
   b. Bat wrangling (X)
   c. Homework (Z)
   d. Naming the bunnies on the palace grounds (W)

9. ON THE DAY OF YOUR CORONATION, YOUR FIRST WORDS ARE:
   a. "The world is mine!" (X)
   b. "Let the fun begin!" (Y)
   c. "This crown is pinching my head." (W)
   d. "OK, now what do I do?" (Z)

10. YOU THINK THAT YOUR LIFE IS:
   a. Boring (Z)
   b. Hilarious (Y)
   c. Beautiful (W)
   d. Unique (X)

11. IN THE SUMMER, YOU:
   a. Visit mermaid friends at camp (Y)
   b. Suntan on the roof of the palace (W)
   c. Wear a cloak (X)
   d. Lounge by the pool (Z)

12. IN THE WINTER, YOU:
   a. Collect dead roses (X)
   b. Make earrings out of icicles (Y)
   c. Take sleigh rides driven by Pegasus (W)
   d. Keep warm at the mall (Z)

13. YOUR ASTROLOGICAL SIGN IS:
   a. Unicorn ascendant in Clouds (X)
   b. Lamb ascendant in Gazelle (W)
   c. Hippopotamus ascendant in Hydrangeas (Y)
   d. Orangutan descendant in pigs' feet (Z)

14. YOU BELIEVE IN:
   a. Wishing on a star (Y)
   b. Santa Claus (W)
   c. Nothing (Z)
   d. Your divine right to rule (X)

15. YOUR LADY-IN-WAITING TALKS TO YOU LIKE:
   a. You're a queen (W)
   b. Your head is in the clouds (Y)
   c. She no longer speaks to you (X)
   d. You do not have a lady-in-waiting—yet. (Z)

16. SOMETIMES, LIFE GOES:
   a. Wowzer (Y)
   b. Meh (Z)
   c. Wheee! (W)
   d. Uh-oh (X)

17. YOUR FAVORITE WORD IS:
   a. Lucullan (W)
   b. Flibbertigibbet (Y)
   c. Defenestrate (X)
   d. Epeolatry (Z)
   (Note: a true princess makes the dictionary her friend)

18. YOUR BEST FRIEND IS:
   a. Totally sweet (W)
   b. Totally boring (Z)
   c. Totally crazy (Y)
   d. Totally in hiding (X)

19. **AT NIGHT, THE STRANGE SOUND YOU HEAR IS:**
   a. Fairy footsteps (Y)
   b. Mice (Z)
   c. The queen snoring (W)
   d. Crocodiles in the moat (X)

20. **PRINCESS EELIZABETH SAID:**
   a. "This water's cold." (Z)
   b. "Water is a dress which cannot be worn." (W)
   c. "Water is wet." (Y)
   d. "Water is my ship." (X)

21. **AT NIGHT YOU DREAM OF:**
   a. A land far away (Y)
   b. A golden palace (W)
   c. A long dark hallway (X)
   d. Forgetting to wear pants to school (Z)

22. **YOU IDENTIFY WITH THE FOLLOWING QUOTATION:**
   a. "All styles are good except the tiresome sort." (Y)
   b. "Wonders are many." (W)
   c. "Curiouser and curiouser." (X)
   d. "They misunderestimated me." (Z)

23. **YOUR PRINCESS CODENAME IS:**
   a. The Evildoer (X)
   b. You've forgotten (Z)
   c. Tra-La-La (W)
   d. The Powdered Sugar Princess (Y)

24. **YOUR SUMMER PALACE IS MADE OF:**
   a. Gold (W)
   b. Candy (Y)
   c. Mirrors (X)
   d. Aluminum siding (Z)

If you answered mostly W:
Without a doubt, you are the most tender princess.

Like Princess Thimbelina, you are a real treasure. Sweet, elegant, and refined like Princess For-a-Day, you love dazzling palaces, charming princes, and enchanted forests.

You dance like a queen, unicorns tell you all their secrets, and your feet never hurt, even after wearing high heels all day. Your friends envy you. In short, everyone adores you.

Be careful, however, not to take after Princess Molly Coddle. There is a sulking seat reserved in her name in her boudoir, since she makes regular use of it. It would be a pity if you spent a lot of your time there.

Also beware of Offal the Awful, the ogre who always hangs around on the look-out for tasty morsels. He flatters anyone who will listen to his compliments. Pay no attention to him. Think about Princess Do-Re-Mi and her sister Fa-Sol-La, who are beautiful, sweet, and elegant without being silly.

If you answered mostly X:
We can see behind your veil. You are a mysterious princess.

You cannot stand any mushiness or baby talk. You dream of becoming like Princess Sticky-Fingers or the Faceless Princess. The Night Princess is your heroine.

You adore black. Your palace is a mansion where you scheme from morning till night.

You can sometimes be a little aloof like the frosty Princess Ices. But you also have secret joys which you studiously enter in your book of secrets: how to make the special fertilizer for your carnivorous plants, how to make particularly disgusting grimaces, and the formulas for extremely effective poisons.

Be careful, however, not to end up like Princess Primandproper: lonely and consumed with meanness.

The night is your best time. You love to watch shooting stars, to sit outside and watch the full moon, and to speak with the bats flying above the palace. But don't stay shut up indoors all day. Daytime also has its own secrets.

If you answered mostly Y:
You are a whimsical princess.

Like the Princess of the Disorient, you are a bit scatterbrained and everyone thinks you are very funny. You mistake up for down, mix up salt and pepper, and confuse north and south.

The slightest nonsense makes you laugh, and like Princess Babbling Brooke, you tell lots of silly stories.

Be careful not to lose your head like Princess Oblivia. When absurdity threatens to take over, put your feet back on the ground and just be happy.

Don't forget, you are not a jester but the king's daughter! Make others laugh with you, but not at you. Do not let others choose the prince you will marry; choose one that you love. Be crazy about him!

If you answered mostly Z:
You are a fake princess.

This test is reserved for true princesses. Once you have finished reading these lines, you will transform into an old polecat, a kangaroo rat, or a used doormat. Your choice.

PROVERBS

Beware of sl**eeping** princesses.
>   (proverb by the Brothers Grimm)

When you chase two princesses at the same time, you won't catch either.
>   (Italian proverb)

The wise man avoids the angry goose.
>   (Chinese proverb)

An eating princess cannot talk.
>   (Prussian proverb)

It only takes one princess to make a party.
>   (Greek proverb)

The generous princess does not fear old age.
>   (Irish proverb)

Never approach a princess in a sulking seat.
>   (wise proverb)

Don't complain that a princess is too beautiful.
>   (Belgian proverb)

I have plenty of apples and pears, but I want only strawberries.
>   (strange proverb)

True queens do not fear young princesses.
>   (New York City proverb)

Princesses are contagious.
>   (Surrealist proverb)

Do not look a gift prince in the mouth.
>   (West African proverb)

A frog prince cannot hide his true nature.
>   (Turkish proverb)

It is a mistake to confuse bad behavior with personality.
(Scottish proverb)

There is a crown for every head.
(Siamese proverb)

A small princess may be great of heart.
(Armenian proverb)

An overworked princess drinks her tea with a fork.
(Indian proverb)

A talking princess doesn't cry.
(Yiddish proverb)

A rolling princess is utterly exhausted.
(stupid proverb)

GLOSSARY

In order to avoid all misunderstandings, one should know certain words and expressions used by princesses.

Here are some key terms:

To be a princess = to sulk
To break a slipper = to make a mistake
Shepherdess = a rival; competitor
To have a toad on the stove = to be rushed, to be late
To lose your blue oak = to be disoriented, lost
A silver-gloved discount = theft
To fall to the bottom of a well = to feel hopeless
To find one's frog = to fall in love
To wear the hat = to be crowned queen

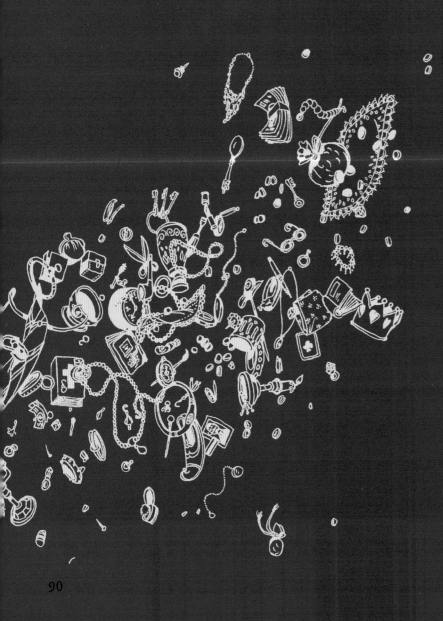

BIBLIOGRAPHY

For those who would like to learn more, here are several important reference works:

The Art of the Sulk, by Princess Molly Coddle

Royal Cuisine or How to Prepare a Princess: Twenty Simple and Savory Recipes, by Offal the Awful

How to Sleep for Years and Still Stay in Shape, by Sleeping Beauty

My Dance Card Is Full, by Princess Tangra-la

A Treasury of Princesses: A Catalogue with Commentary, from the Queens Museum of Princesses

The Future of Princesses, by Princess Claire Voyant

What Unicorns Have Told Me, by Anonymous

The Lives of the Princesses, Volumes I, II, and III, by Princess Paige

Attics of the World: A Comprehensive Guide, by the Night Princess

Recipes from the Archduchess, by Princess Buffet, Member of the Order of the La-di-dah

The Royal Orchestra and Its Instruments, by Maestro Tempo Moderato

Index